Caribou Song

Ateek Oonagamoon / Atihko Nikamon

"Atihko Nikamon" is high Cree. "Ateek Oonagamoon" is a local dialect of that high Cree. The English equivalent would be like the difference between "I am going to try" and "I'm gonna try." But both titles mean "Caribou Song."

Published in Canada by Fifth House Ltd., 195 Allstate Parkway, Markham, Ontario L3R 4T8
Published in the United States by Fifth House Ltd., 311 Washington Street, Brighton, Massachusetts 02135

www.fifthhousepublishers.ca

10 9 8 7 6 5 4 3 2 1

Library and Archives Canada Cataloguing in Publication
Highway, Tomson, 1951-
     Caribou song / Tomson Highway ; illustrations by John Rombough = Ateek oonagamoon / Atihko nikamon / Tomson Highway ; os isopéhikéwina John Rombough.
Previously published: Markham, Ont.: Fifth House Publishers, 2012.
Text in English and Cree.
ISBN 978-1-927083-49-9 (paperback)
1. Rombough, John, illustrator II. Title. III. Title: Ateek oonagamoon/Atihko nikamon.
PS8565.I433C37 2016   jC813'.54   C2016-903465-8

Publisher Cataloging-in-Publication Data (U.S.)
Highway, Tomson, 1951-, author. | Rombough, John, illustrator.
     Caribou song / Tomson Highway ; illustrator by John Rombough.
Markham, Ontario ; Fifth House Publishers, 2016 | Summary: In this tale set in northern Manitoba and told in English and Cree, brothers Joe and Cody go searching for the ateek (caribou) and become part of a magical adventure" - provided by publisher.
ISBN: 978-1-927083-499 (paperback)
Caribou – Juvenile fiction. | Folklore – Canada – Juvenile fiction. | Tales – Canada – Juvenile Fiction. | BISAC: JUVENILE FICTION / Fairy Tales & Folklore / Country & Ethnic.
LCC Pz8.1H544.Ca | DDC 398.209 – dc23

Fifth House Ltd. acknowledges with thanks the Canada Council for the Arts, and the Ontario Arts Council for their support of our publishing program. We acknowledge the financial support of the Government of Canada for our publishing activities.

Cover illustration by John Rombough
Manufactured in China by Sheck Wah Tong Printing Press Ltd.

Caribou Song

TOMSON HIGHWAY

Illustrations by **John Rombough**

Ateek Oonagamoon / Atihko Nikamon

TOMSON HIGHWAY

Osisopéhikéwina **John Rombough**

FIFTH
HOUSE

Joe and Cody lived with their mama, their papa, and Cody's black dog, Ootsie. They lived too far north for most trees. Most of the year the lakes and islands and rivers and hills were covered in snow.

Joe igwa Cody kaageeweechaa-amaachik maana oomaamaa-waawa igwa oopaapaawaawa igwa Cody oocheemsisa Ootsie. Waathow keeweet'nook kaageeweegichik ita keegaach kaapaskwaathik. Kwayus mistaa-i maana koona kee-apithoowa ooma maana kaapipoonthik, saagahiganeek, minstigook, seepeek, waacheek, poogweetee.

All year long, they followed the caribou with a sled pulled by eight huskies. "Mush!" Papa would yell, and the dogs would run straight forward. "Cha!" he would shout, and they would turn right. And when he yelled "U!" they turned left.

Kapee-pipoon maana ateegwa keep' mitsaaweewuk ootaapaanaaskwa meena eye-naanao atimwuk ee-aapacheeyaachik. "Mush!" kaateepweet maana paapaa, igwa aspin sipweepaatawuk maana anee-i atimwuk. "Cha!" kaateepweet maana paapaa igwa atimwuk micheechineek iteegee maana taa-ispaataawuk. Igwa keespin "u" teepwao paapaa, neetee iteegee nawach maana taa-ispaataawuk.

Joe played the accordion, the kitoochigan. From morning to night he played and sang, "Ateek, ateek! Astum, astum! Yo-ah, ho-ho! Caribou, caribou! Come, come! Yo-ah, ho-ho!"

Kwayus oogitoochigana maana tagitoochigao Joe. Aaskow kapee-geesik maana tagitoochigao igwa tanagamoo. "Ateek, ateek! Astum, astum! Yoa-ho-ho!" taa-isinagamoo maana.

And from morning to night Cody danced. He danced
on the rocks, he danced on the ice, he even danced under
the full silver moon.

Igwa Cody weetha taneemee-itoo. Taagooch asineek
tanee-mee-itoo, taagooch maskwameek, aapoo ataameek
tip'skaa-ipeesimook maana taneemee-itoo.

One day, at the end of May, the family stopped on an island. After a lunch of whitefish and bannock, Joe and Cody wandered off and found a meadow surrounded by forest. In the middle stood a great big rock.

"Cody," said Joe. "This is the perfect spot. Let's sing and dance for the caribou. You dance with your arms up like antlers. I'll sing 'Ateek, ateek' and play kitoochigan. And before you know it, ten thousand caribou will burst out of the forest."

Peeyugoo-geesigow oosooma meena eeseegwanthik kaagipeecheeyaachik ootaapaanaaskoowow peeyuk minstigook achithow tameech'soochik kichi. Ispeek eegeemoowaachik ateegameegwa meena paagweesigana, Joe igwa Cody kaageen-tay-papaamooteechik noochimeek ita aapeetow eetawaathik kaageem'skawaachik mistasineeya.

"Cody," Joe kaa-itweet, "oota maawachi mithawsin. Oota kitoochigeetaan igwa nagamootaan igwa neemee-itootaan ateegwuk kichi. Nemee-itoo keetha ateek ooteeskana taaskooch taa-isimichiminaman kispitoona igwa neetha nagitoochigaan k'sik nanagamoon, "ateek, ateek." Igoosi isi meecheet ateegwuk seemaak tatagoopaataawuk."

So Cody raised his arms to look like antlers, and began to dance. He lifted his left moccasin, then his right. Then his left, and then, *oof!* There he was, flat on a tuft of pillow-soft caribou moss poking through the melting snow.

Igwaani Cody oopinam igwa oospitoona ateek ooteeskana taa-isinaagwanthigi igwa sipwee-neemee-itoo. Oopinam neegaan peeyuk oosit igweespeek kootuk igweespeek keetawm animeethoo n'stum igweespeek, oof! Keepaagisin isa. Kitaatawee igoota moochik kaacheepatapit ita apisees aski kaanooganthik kooneek oochi.

"Ateek, ateek! Astum, astum!" Joe played and sang as Cody got up and danced like a young caribou. They were so busy dancing and singing and playing kitoochigan that they didn't hear the rumbling.

"Ateek, ateek! Astum, astum!" kaanagamoot Joe igwa kaagitoochigeet. Igwa Cody weetha keetawm kaaneepawit igwa keetawm kaaneemee-itoot taskooch acheegoosis taa-isinaagoosit. Ithigook soogi eenagamoochik k'sik eegitoochigeechik k'sik eeneemee-itoochik mawch apoochiga peetam'wuk animeethoo keegwaathoo kaageetipeetagwanthik.

Mama and Papa were sitting near the fire, drinking tea.

"Thunder?" Mama asked Papa. "In May?"

"Can't be," said Papa. "Not until summer."

"Then what can it—" But Mama never finished her question.

Meegwaach igoospeek k'soowaak kwatawaaneek n'seegaach l'tee keeyaapich maa-minigweewuk oomaamaawaawa igwa oopaapaawaawa.

"Oogitoowuk?" kaagagweechimaat maamaa ooweegimaagana, eepeetak weesta animeethoo keegwaathoo. "Mootha chee keeyaapich seegwan?"

"Mootha itigwee oogitoowuk, waat'stagaach," kaa-itweet paapaa, "kaaneepik ooma maana poogoo peetagoosiwuk oogitoowuk."

"Keegway maa-a anima…" kaatee-itweet maamaa. Mawch maa-a apoochiga kaskeetow tageesee-ayamit.

Faster than lightning, a thousand caribou burst from the forest. Two thousand caribou ran between the cooking fire and the boys. Ten thousand caribou filled the meadow like a lake.

Kitaatawee meecheet ateegwuk kaapeematawisi-paataachik noochimeek oochi. Mitooni itigwee neesoo m'taa-atoo m'taa-atoo m'tanow ateegwuk kitaatawee pimpaataawuk aapeetow kwataawaaneek igwa ita anee-i neesoo naapees'suk keeyaapich kaameetaweethit. Apoochiga nawach awasimee atimeecheetoowuk anee-i ateegwuk, kaagithow soogi eepimpaataachik.

Joe stood in the middle of the plunging caribou. Through the tangle of their rushing legs and antlers, he could just see Cody, small as a doll, sitting on the caribou moss.

Joe took one step, then another, as if swimming through the snorting, steaming bodies, until he reached his brother.

Igoota neepaa-oo Joe mitooni aapeetow ita kaapimpaataathit anee-i ateegwa. Igwa igoota oochi igwa kaawaap'maat Codeewa, ee-apithit moochik, taagooch askeeya, ee-apiseesisit, taaskooch peechaa-ik anee-i ateegwa ooskaatiwantheek igwa ooteeskawantheek eeyayaat, eepimithaat.

N'seegaach kaatinaataat ooseem'sa Joe, taaskooch ataameek nipeek eep'maatagaat, iskook kaa-ooteetawaat.

When he took Cody's hand they seemed to float right through the herd. The next thing they knew they were perched on the big rock, Cody on Joe's lap, kitoochigan between them. All they could see were antlers. And all they could hear were hooves, drumming all around them like thunder.

"Ateek, ateek! Astum, astum!" Joe sang again. "Caribou, caribou! Come, come!"

Ispeek peeyuk Cody oocheechi ee-ootinak Joe, eesneesichik naapees'suk igwa kaatip'mooteechik. Mitooni taaskooch kwayus n'seegaach eepimithaachik, ateegwuk pooweetee aa-itow weeyaa-oowaak eepimpaataathichik. Iskook mistasineek kaatagooseegwow igwa igoota taagooch kaacheepatapichik. Cody taagootapoo Joe ooskaatithoowa, oogitoochigana keeyaapich eetaagoonaat Joe. Igwa poogweetee kaaganawaapichik, ateegwuk ooteeskanthoowow poogoo kaawaap'maachik. Ateek oositiwaawa meena poogoo peetam'wuk, taaskooch oogitoowuk eeteetaagoosinthichik.

"Ateek, ateek! Astum, astum!" kaanagamoot Joe. "Ateek, ateek! Astum, astum!"

And out of the drumming came the voice of the herd,
whispering and moaning and wailing as it flowed past the rock.

"Cody! Joe!" it said. "Come, come!" And the boys opened
their arms to embrace the spirit.

Igweespeek igoota oochi igwa kaatipeetaagwow kootuk
keegwaathoo anee-i neesoo naapees'suk, taaskooch peechaa-ik
ateegook oochi awinuk n'seegaach eenagamoostamaagoochik.

"Cody! Joe!" kaanagamoot ana awinuk. "Astum, astum!"
Nanseegaach kaa-iti-oopinaagwow oospitooniwaawa
anee-i neesoo naapees'suk, taaskooch eeweentay-ag-
waskit'naachik anee-i awithoowa.

When the river of caribou had become a trickle, the brothers heard another wailing sound. Mama's face was buried in Papa's parka.

"Woof, woof!" Ootsie danced around the great big rock. "Ho-ho!" Papa sang out. But when Mama looked up at Papa's face, she didn't see tears but a smile as bright as the sun.

⬭

Ispeek kaagithow kaanamaateethit igwa igaa awasimee kaapeetagoosinthit anee-i ateegwa, kootuk keegwaathoo igwa kaatipeetaagwow anee-i neesoo naapees'suk. Oomaamaawa isa, eemaatoothit, weegwaagan keeyaapich eegaataat ooweegimaa-gaanthoowa ooskootaagwantheek, eeteetheetak ateegwuk isa eegeen'paa-iskaawaachik eesneesichik oogoosisa.

"Woof! Woof!" kaamiksimoot Ootsie k'sik kaapapaami-gwaaskootit mistasineek waaskwow.

"Ho-ho!" kaateepweet paapaa. Maa-a ispeek kaganawaap'maat oonaapeema maamaa, mawch kaamatoothit. Kaapaapithit poogoo.

For there, atop the large rock, sat Joe and Cody, laughing and laughing and laughing.

Athis igoota taagooch mistasineek kaacheep-atapichik Joe ekwa Cody, eemichimintoochik igwa eepaapichik igwa eepaapichik igwa eepaapichik.

TOMSON HIGHWAY is an award-winning playwright and the author of
The Rez Sisters, Dry Lips Oughta Move to Kapuskasing, Rose, and *Kiss of
the Fur Queen*. He was made a member of the Order of Canada in 1994.
Originally from Manitoba, he now lives in northern Ontario when he is
not travelling abroad.

TOMSON HIGHWAY ana nihithowi-masinaa-igao kaageemaasinaa-ak
masina-igana *The Rez Sisters, Dry Lips Oughta Move to Kapuskasing,
Rose*, igwa *Kiss of the Fur Queen*. Order of Canada keemeethow 1994.
Manitoba kaageeneetaaweegit, keeweetnook Ontario igwa weegoo ispeek
iga maana kaapmootee-oot poogweetee.

JOHN ROMBOUGH's painting style reflects the harmony of the Dene
peoples. As a professional artist for over a decade, he has seen his work
featured across Canada, including at the 2010 Olympic Games. He lives
with his family in the small community of Lutselk'e on the eastern shore of
Great Slave Lake in the Northwest Territories. This is his first picture book.

JOHN ROMBOUGH oos'soopeegaa-igana athimoomeewuk maana kapee
ootooteema Dene kaa-isitheegaasoochik itinoowuk. Aspin awasimee
mitaa-at aski igwa kaagees'soopeegaa-igeet. Poogweetee igwa meena kwayus
waapaatathoogeewanaw anee-i oos'soopeegaa-igana, apoochiga itee Olympic
Games kaageemeetawaagaaniwagwaw 2010. Waasagaam Great Slave Lake
kaa-ichigaateek misti-saagaa-igan kaaweegit ootooteema asichi ootee waathow
keeweetinook Northwest Territories kaa-isitheegaateek anima aski. Lutselk'e
isitheegaatao anima ooteenow ita kaaweegit. Oomeethoo maasinaa-igan
mawachi n'stum kaagee-ooseetaat.